PUFFIN BOOKS

THE QUEEN'S BIRTHDAY HAT

Margaret Ryan lives in a creaky old house in Scotland with her husband, two children and a dog. She was a teacher before she became a full-time writer. She writes funny stories about school, fairy godmothers, pirates, witches, kings and queens, monsters, animals, plumbers and police officers. In fact, about anything that makes her laugh. Her hobbies are walking her big hairy dog called Hanibal, and playing the piano – though not usually at the same time. Her family don't think much of her piano playing. When she starts, they all go to the far end of the house, closing all the doors behind them. But Hanibal stays. He lies under the piano, puts his big paws over his floppy ears, and howls.

Margaret Ryan

The Queen's Birthday Hat

Illustrated by Priscilla Lamont

PUFFIN BOOKS

PUFFIN BOOKS

Published by the Penguin Group
Penguin Books Ltd, 80 Strand, London WC2R, 0RL, England
Penguin Putnam Inc., 375 Hudson Street, New York, New York 10014, USA
Penguin Books Australia Ltd, 250 Camberwell Road, Camberwell, Victoria 3124, Australia
Penguin Books Canada Ltd, 10 Alcorn Avenue, Toronto, Ontario, Canada M4V 3B2
Penguin Books India (P) Ltd, 11 Community Centre, Panchsheel Park, New Delhi – 110 017, India
Penguin Books (NZ) Ltd, Cnr Rosedale and Airborne Roads, Albany, Auckland, New Zealand
Penguin Books (South Africa) (Pty) Ltd, 24 Sturdee Avenue, Rosebank 2196, South Africa

Penguin Books Ltd, Registered Offices: 80 Strand, London WC2R, 0RL, England

www.penguin.com

Published in Puffin Books 1999
Published in this edition 2001
5 7 9 10 8 6

Set in 15 on 22pt Times New Roman Schoolbook

Printed in China by Midas Printing Ltd

British Library Cataloguing in Publication Data
A CIP catalogue record for this book is available from the British Library

ISBN 0–141–31301–3

It was a week till Queen
Forgetmenot's birthday.

1

"What would you like for your birthday, my dear?" asked King Forgetalot over breakfast.

"Sausages," said the queen.

"Sausages? For your birthday?"

"No, sausages for my breakfast. Where are they? We always have sausages on Tuesdays. Have the pets run off with them again?"

"Never mind the sausages," said
the king. "What would you like for
your birthday?"

The queen thought for a moment.
"I know what I don't want," she
said.

"I don't want
any more
furry
slippers
for the dog to chew or any more
lacy tights for the cat to claw."

"No more slippers or tights,"
muttered King Forgetalot, making a
note.

"And I
don't want
any more
silky cushions
for the goat to eat or
another feather boa.
The donkey is still
wearing my
last one."

"No more cushions
or feather boas,"
muttered the
king, making
another
note.

"And I don't want any more fancy necklaces. The parrot pecks them, and scatters the beads everywhere. Then I skid on them and fall on the floor."

"No more fancy necklaces," muttered the king, nearly filling his notepad.

"I know what I do want," said
Queen Forgetmenot. "I want a new
garden hat. One that will keep the
sun out of my eyes when I'm
planting out the marigolds or
chasing the blackbirds off the runner
beans."

"A new hat!" cried the king.
"Splendid! I'll telephone the royal
hatters right away before I forget!"

Four hours later, in the middle of lunch, the royal hatters arrived to measure the queen's head for her birthday hat.

The queen looked up at Mr Topper, Mrs Bonnet and Miss Stetson.

"I don't suppose you brought any sausages?" she said.

The three hatters shook their heads
and got out their tape-measures.

"It shall be my greatest pleasure
to make the most magnificent hat in
all the kingdom for your majesty,"
said Mr Topper, bowing low.

"It doesn't have to be all that
magnificent," said the queen.

"No, it shall be my greatest pleasure to make the most wonderful hat in all the world for your majesty," said Mrs Bonnet, bowing lower.

"It doesn't have to be all that wonderful," said the queen.

"No, no, it shall be my greatest
pleasure to make the most
stupendous hat in all the universe
for your majesty," said Miss
Stetson, bowing so low she fell over
and bumped her nose.

"Oh, get on with it then," said the
queen, who was by now wishing
she'd asked for a new spade instead.

11

Two days later, in the middle of tea, the three hatters came back.

First came Mr Topper

carrying the tallest hatbox Queen
Forgetmenot had ever seen.

"Got a giraffe in there?" she
asked.

Mr Topper shook his head and
pulled out of the box a hat shaped
like a skyscraper. It was blue and
pink and had little windows made of
coloured glass, and a working lift.

"Now what do you think of
that?"

"Magnificent," said King
Forgetalot.

"Do I wear it or live in
it?" asked Queen
Forgetmenot.

Next came Mrs Bonnet carrying the widest hatbox the queen had ever seen.

"Got a rhino in there?" she asked.

Mrs Bonnet shook her head and drew out of the box a hat shaped like a flying saucer. It had a clear glass dome with little green plastic men working inside.

"Now what
do you
think of
that?"

"Wonderful," said
King Forgetalot.
"Do I wear it or
ly in it?" asked
Queen Forgetmenot.

Finally came Miss Stetson
carrying a zigzag-shaped hatbox.

"I give up," said the queen.
"What have you got in there?"

Miss Stetson smiled and said,
"The idea came to me in a flash."

And she drew out of the box the
tiniest black hat on which stood a
gigantic metal
zigzag of lightning.

"Now
what do you
think of
that?"

"Stupendous,"
said King Forgetalot.

"Stupid," muttered Queen Forgetmenot.

"And now Queen Forgetmenot will choose which hat she wants for her birthday," beamed the king.

But the queen wasn't happy. She whispered in the king's ear. "These hats are hopeless. I said I wanted a garden hat. Didn't you make a note? Tell these mad hatters to go away. Tell them to scoot, vanish, hop it. Right now."

"Right you are, my dear," sighed the king.

He turned to the three hatters who were by now quarrelling among themselves as to whose hat was best.

"My hat was best."

"No, my hat was best."

"Rubbish. My hat was definitely best."

"The queen," interrupted King Forgetalot, "wishes to thank you very much. She thinks all the hats are so splendid she just can't choose. She would like you to go away and come back with a garden hat that the three of you have made together."

"That's not what I told you to say," muttered the queen.

"Wasn't it?" said the king. "I should have made a note."

Four days later, on the very day of the queen's birthday, the three hatters came back. They arrived before breakfast carrying the tallest, widest hatbox the queen had ever seen.

"Now," beamed the king. "I'm sure this will be something special. I hope you like it, my dear."

The three
hatters smiled,
opened up the
box and took
out the
queen's
birthday hat.

It was shaped like a pine tree. On
it hung pears, plums, peaches,
apples, apricots and bananas, as
well as garlands of forget-me-nots.

The queen's mouth opened in
astonishment.

"I knew you'd like it, my dear,"
beamed the king. "It's a real garden
hat."

"It's very nice," said the queen.
"Thank you very much. I shall wear
it into the garden this very minute."

The king paid the three hatters and the queen went out into the garden. She put her fingers to her lips and gave a loud whistle. All the pets came running – the dog, the cat, the goat, the donkey and the parrot.

They gathered round the queen to gaze at her new hat.

"Fancy hat. Fancy hat," squawked the parrot.

"This," said Queen Forgetmenot, "is my birthday hat. It's not quite the garden hat I wanted so I'm making you a present of it."

She took the hat off and put it on the ground.

"There you are," she said. "You may eat my hat."

The pets tucked in but, as they did, the queen spied the donkey's hat. It was a plain straw hat with a wide brim. She tried it on her own head. It fitted perfectly.

"Just what I wanted for my birthday," she said. "Now all I need is some breakfast."

"Coming, my dear," said the king. "I've brought your birthday breakfast on a tray and look what's on it."

"At last," said the queen. "Sausages!"